Fearless

by

Daniel Morden

Illustrated by Peter Clover

For Alex and Evan

First published in 2009 in Great Britain by
Barrington Stoke Ltd
18 Walker St, Edinburgh, EH3 7LP

www.barringtonstoke.co.uk

ISBN: 978-1-84299-660-7

Printed in Great Britain by Bell & Bain Ltd

Contents

Chapter 1

The Son Who Could Do Nothing

Once upon a time there was a farmer who had two sons.

One son – the oldest – could do everything.

The other son – the youngest – could do nothing. His father sat him by the fire. That way his father always knew where he was.

Day after day the boy would stare into the fire, and watch the flames dance.

****

One day the father called to his oldest son, the one who could do everything, "I need you to take a note to your uncle. If you leave now you'll be at his farm by midnight."

The oldest brother backed away.

"Father, if I go now I'll have to walk past *that* house in the dark. The House of the Devil. And after the stories I've heard about the things people have seen inside that house – when I walk past it in the daytime I'm afraid. But to walk past it at night ... that would make me shudder with fear!"

The youngest son, the one who sat by the fire, looked up. He stared at his brother. He muttered, "Shudder ... Fear ..."

A few days later the father sat the two of them down and said, "Soon you'll be old enough to choose a job by which you'll make your living. What do you want to learn?"

The oldest son said, "I've been thinking ... I want to learn how to be a farmer like you."

"Good," said the father. He looked down at his youngest son, the one by the fire.

"And you ...?"

"I've been thinking too ... I want to learn how to shudder with fear!"

"What?" said the father.

"Everyone talks about it but I don't know what it means. Until I learn how to shudder with fear I won't feel grown up. I won't be complete."

The father said, "What – did I do – to deserve you?!"

Chapter 2
His First Murder

A few days later the father was walking, kicking stones, when he saw the church. There was a man outside, raking the dead leaves from between the graves. He was the caretaker. The father opened the gate, went up to the old man, and said, "Can you help me? I have a son, and he told me he wanted to learn how to shudder with fear. What if I send him to church tonight. You could wait for him in the shadows, and in the middle of the night when everything is still and silent, you can teach him how to shudder with fear!"

The old man grinned.

Then the father went home. His youngest son was sitting by the fire as always.

The father said, "Hey!"

The boy looked up.

"You know the caretaker of the church? He just died. We can't bury him now, it's too dark. So we put his body on a table in the church. Someone has to sit by the corpse, keep watch over the body all night long. Someone has to be a mourner. You're going to do it."

A huge grin spread across the boy's face. He said, "My training begins!"

He stood up and went to the kitchen. He thought, *What do they eat in church? Bread. What do they drink in church? Wine.*

So he grabbed a loaf of bread and a bottle of wine and set off, shambling along the road. He took the cork out of the bottle with his teeth and gulped down the wine. He tore off a hunk of bread and chewed it messily.

It was dark. The bushes snagged and ripped at his sleeve as he passed. The forest was full of strange sounds. Red eyes followed him between the trees. There was the hill. On top of the hill, looming over the road, was the church. All around it, grave-stones leaned toward one another as if they were children, whispering secrets.

The boy didn't notice.

He got to the gate of the grave-yard – it opened with a creak. He stumbled between the graves. He pushed open the door of the church.

Inside, the only light came from candles. Above him and around him was as black as silence. He walked down the middle of the church until he saw a circle of candles. Inside the circle there was a table.

On the table there was a white sheet, like a shroud. He could see a shape under the sheet, the shape of a man.

The boy thought, *I've never seen a dead person before ... perhaps that'll make me shudder with fear*. He lifted up the sheet and took a look. He was still chewing as he did so.

The old man hiding under the sheet could hear a sloppy sound. A little blob of wet bread flew out of the boy's open mouth and landed on the end of the old man's nose ... but the old man didn't move. He thought, *In a*

minute – *I'm going to give him the fright of his life!*

The boy put down the sheet thinking, *No ... that didn't make me shudder with fear.*

He carried on eating the bread, until he'd finished the bread, and he carried on drinking the wine, until he'd finished the wine. He'd never had wine before. He was drunk. He walked around the church, staggering, hiccupping, burping, swinging the bottle. The old man hiding under the sheet got angry. He thought, *The young of today have no respect for the dead. I won't bother trying to frighten him, I will jump up and tell him off!*

So he threw off the sheet, sat up and looked around. The boy had his back to the old man. The old man leaped off the table, ran over to the boy and grabbed his arm. The boy turned around.

The old man said, "Mourners shouldn't be drunk!"

"And the dead shouldn't be alive!" Bam! The boy hit him on the head with the bottle.

****

The next day, the boy's father entered the church. He saw his son sitting with a bottle by his knee. And there in front of him, spread out on the floor, the caretaker, with a purple lump on his fore-head.

His father said, "You've killed him!"

"Well, you said he was dead, but he wasn't dead, so I made him dead. What's the matter?"

"I don't want to know what you did. You take these coins and in return I'll take back the family name. I want nothing more to do with you. You are not of my family any more.

You can do what you want. You can go where you like. But you can't come home."

Weeping, the father walked out of the church.

The boy stared at the coins on the floor.

"OK." He picked up the coins. "I'm going to learn how to shudder with fear. That's what I'm going to do!"

Chapter 3
The Hanging Tree

Off he went, following the path. Every time he met someone he would say, "Hey, could you teach me how to shudder with fear?"

And they'd look at him and frown and shake their heads.

But then when he asked one man, the man stopped and said, "Why would you want to learn such a thing? If you really want to, then not far from here there's a hill. On the top of the hill there is a gallows, a Hanging Tree. From every branch there hangs a corpse, a dead body. If you spend the night under the tree by the morning you will know what fear is!"

"Thank you, my friend!" said the boy. "Which way?"

"Ah, you must go ...

Down this lonely road,

Past Sucking Pit,

Turn left at The Cave of Doom,

Through Gloomy Hollow,

Round Dark Moon Pool,

Over Grab Ankle Bridge,

Across old Jenny Green-teeth's yard.

Then you'll see them. The dead bodies on the Hanging Tree. Dancing to the song of the wind!"

The boy replied, "Perfect. Meet you there in the morning!"

So off he went.

He waved at the ravens on the lonely road,

Lost a shoe in the Sucking Pit,

Shouted "Hallooo!" into The Cave of Doom,

Bumped into a Beastie in Gloomy Hollow,

Skimmed a stone on Dark Moon Pool,

Lost the other shoe on Grab Ankle Bridge,

Petted the growling hound in old Jenny Green-teeth's yard.

Then he saw the Hanging Tree.

Crows rose from the branches into the grey sky.

The wind stirred the corpses. They twisted on their ropes.

The boy said, "You up there! Can you teach me what fear is? Can you teach me how to shudder?"

The corpses did not reply.

"Well, if you won't speak to me now, I'll wait until you answer!"

The shadows swelled. All at once he found he could see the stars.

He lit a fire. The wind played with the bodies like children on swings.

He looked up.

"You up there! I'm cold down here even with the fire, so you lot must be freezing! Come down and get warm! Let me help you!"

He climbed up the trunk of the tree.

He pulled out a knife and Bump! a corpse fell to the ground beside the fire. Bump! Bump!

At last all the bodies lay in a clump. Flies wandered over their faces, into their nostrils, and mouths, and ears. The hang-man had left his autograph: a bright bruise on every neck, purple and yellow and crimson.

He sat the corpses in a circle, each lazy head against another's shoulder. He shuffled in amongst them and said, "Do you know any songs?"

He sang every song he knew. The rats, chittering and chewing and nibbling at the

cold flesh, seemed to like them. The game of charades was less of a success.

Next morning the man the boy had met on the road came up the hill to see the boy.

The boy stood up. All the corpses flopped back onto the grass.

"Your friends are stupid!" the boy said to the man. "My father thinks I'm useless, but at least when my clothes catch fire I know I have to stop them burning!"

The man looked at the charred clothes on the corpses, the white bones exposed by the rats, and he shivered. The stench made him gag.

"If this hasn't taught you how to shudder with fear, there's one last place you can try. Not far from here there's a house. The house is infested with evil things. They call it The House of the Devil. No man or woman has ever spent the night in that house without being driven mad by the next morning, so vile and shocking are the sights within. If anyone can spend the night and feel no fear they will banish the ghosts. The princess of this country wants the house as a summer palace. She has offered a reward in the hope that someone will rid the house of ghosts. Spend the night there. Either you learn how to shudder with fear or you make your fortune. Both ways you win!"

"Thank you, my friend!" said the boy, and off he went to the palace of the princess.

Chapter 4
The House of the Devil

When the guards heard what he wanted to do, they banged their drums, they blew their horns ...

"Another brave soul wishes to try his luck in The House of the Devil!" they shouted.

The boy was taken in to the throne room ... and there was the Princess.

When he saw her and she saw him, it was love – or something like it.

"What can I do for you?" she said.

"I want to spend the night in the House of the Devil! I want to learn how to shudder with fear!"

"I don't want you to ... I want you to stay here with me."

"I don't want to. I want to learn how to shudder with fear!"

"If I can't talk you out of it ... Is there anything you'd like to have in the house to keep you ... company?"

"Can I have anything?"

She looked him up and down.

"Uh-huh ..."

"Good! I'd like a metal chisel!"

So they gave him a metal chisel and off he went to The House of the Devil.

No grass grew around it. No birds sang. The trees, leafless, stretched up like veins against the night sky.

The house was like a head; the windows eyes, the door a mouth.

The boy didn't notice.

He pushed open the door – of course it creaked ...

At first it was so dark you'd have to shut your eyes to see how dark it was ...

But slowly his eyes became used to the lack of light.

He saw veils of cobwebs everywhere.

He saw at either end of the room a huge fire-place, like a cave.

He saw in the middle of the room a heap of wood that had once been used for a fire. The boy didn't stop to wonder why they hadn't used a fire-place.

Across the room from him he saw an enormous four-poster bed.

The boy lit the wood and waited for something to happen.

At midnight he heard a clatter. Down a chimney fell the top of a man, the ribs, the arms, the hands, the neck, the head ... It hit the fire-place face down. A cloud of ash billowed up into the room.

The hands began to twitch. The head lifted, its leering face covered in a mask of ash. It pulled itself out of the fire-place and across the floor towards the boy.

There came another clatter from the other fire-place. Another cloud of ash rose up. In there the boy saw a waist, a pair of legs, and feet … It pressed against the back wall of the chimney and pushed itself onto the floor, shuffling across the cold stone towards him.

The boy looked at one. He looked at the other.

He said, "Have you met? Legs, this is body, body, this is legs …"

The ghost assembled itself and sat beside him.

Down the chimney fell heads, that bounced toward him. He watched hands scuttle across the floor like spiders, making patterns in the dust, torsos that hopped and legs that shuffled.

The boy said, "Welcome, my friends! Come and sit beside me!"

The boy saw the huge heap of bodies squirm, arms and legs thrashing, eyes rolling in their sockets, mouths gulping and uttering wordless sounds.

Out of the heap the ghosts assembled bit by bit. The boy said, "Wait! You've left some legs behind! And heads! We could play bowling!"

He collected the legs and assembled them in a triangle, like skittles,

One in front,

Two behind the one,

Three behind the two,

Four behind the three ...

Then he picked up one of the heads –

"You, my friend, will be the ball!"

He bowled the head ... it rolled, wobbled and fell over.

He picked it up.

"You're the wrong shape. You should be round. You don't roll properly. You're too rough. Never mind. I have a chisel!"

The head looked at the chisel. The head looked at the boy. The head screamed. The boy made a lunge at the head, there was a flash of light, a puff of smoke and the head had vanished. All the ghosts had gone.

The boy saw two lines of candles leading to a coffin. He walked between the candles. As he passed the candles went out. He lifted the lid of the coffin and saw an old man lying

on his back, as if he was asleep. The boy touched his fore-head.

"You're so cold. Stay there, my friend!"

He ran to the fire and put his hands as close as he could to the flames.

He pressed his fingers against the old man's cheeks.

The old man's skin came off on his fingers, like wet tissue paper.

"Oh, I'm sorry! I've spoilt your face!"

He scooped up the body, carried it across the room, put it in the bed and jumped in next to it, rubbing the skin.

"I'll be your hot water bottle!"

The bed shook. It trembled. It stood up. It fell back. It lifted from the floor.

The bed crashed against the wall. It flew backwards at break-neck speed. It tipped upside down. It righted itself and bucked like a rodeo bull.

The boy, holding on tightly, cheered and yelled, "More! More! Faster!"

The bed crashed to the ground.

The body beside him had changed colour. It was no longer cold, it was warm.

Then it wasn't warm, it was hot.

Then it wasn't hot, it was burning. The sheets were on fire! The boy looked at the face on the pillow beside him and it was the face of the Devil. He was in bed with the Devil!

The Devil laughed. He sat up and began to throttle the boy. His eyes were like blazing

coals, his mouth like a yawning cave, the
teeth like razors.

The boy shouted, "That is the thanks I get for warming you up?"

The Devil stopped.

All of these beings drew strength from fear. If you had no fear, they lost their strength.

The Devil leapt out of bed and grabbed an axe. He lifted it above his head. The boy was quick as thought. He punched the Devil in the face. The Devil dropped the axe and toppled backwards. The boy grabbed the axe with one hand and with the other he grasped the Devil's beard. Bam! The axe hit the beard and the Devil was pinned to the floor. The Devil screamed. The boy grasped the beard with both hands, pulled it out of the hole he'd made, dragged the Devil to the coffin, threw him in, slammed down the lid, sat on it and said, "You're not coming out until you learn how to behave!"

At first the Devil was punching on the under-side of the coffin lid making the boy bounce up and down.

But then the punching became a knocking.

Then the knocking became a tapping.

Then the tapping became a scratching.

And then all was silent.

Chapter 5
I Know What Fear Is

At last the light of the morning came through the window.

The door opened and there was the princess. She said, "Well, did you learn how to shudder with fear?"

"No," said the boy, "Guess who's in here!"

He jumped from the coffin, lifted the lid … and inside there was dust, just dust and ashes.

She said, "You've won! You have banished the ghosts that infested this place. They can never return. I promised a great reward to the one who'd feel no fear in this place. And as it is you, I will give a great reward indeed. Me!"

"I would love to marry you … but the thing is, I can't. You see, I haven't learned how to shudder with fear yet. Until I learn that I won't be grown-up! I won't be any use to you!"

So he resumed his quest. But now he felt different. Wherever he went he kept thinking of her.

So one winter's night he returned to her palace and said, "Although I don't know how to shudder with fear, if you would marry me I would marry you."

So they were married. At the wedding the priest said, "Boy, do you take this princess to be your wife?"

And the boy replied, "Priest, can you teach me how to shudder with fear?"

They were happy, the two of them tried to be kind and thoughtful to one another ... except every day the boy would go on and on about wanting to shudder with fear! The princess grew angry. One night he woke her up. He was talking in his sleep! He kept mumbling, "I just want to shudder with fear ... Shudder!"

She'd had enough. Something snapped inside her. She got out of the bed in her night-dress, put on some shoes and a cloak, walked down the stone staircase, across the snow-covered court-yard, over the draw-bridge to the moat. She picked a great rock and threw it into the moat to crack the ice. She dipped a bucket into the hole she'd made in the ice. She filled the bucket full of ice-cold water. She made her way across the draw-bridge, through the court-yard, up the staircase, she drew back the sheets of the bed, and there he was, curled up like a baby. She threw the ice cold water over him as he slept.

"Aaaaah!" he jumped up.

"Listen to me!" she said. "I love you. But I'm sick of you talking about wanting to shudder with fear! Every day you go on and on. If I hear you say those words I will leave you and you will never see me again!"

The boy looked at her. A long wet eel wiggled down inside his night-shirt. He said, "And I love you. And the thought of you, leaving me ..."

His hands, his arms were trembling –
"Don't leave me! I feel different now that I've
met you! You've changed me! If you were to
go, the world would seem a darker place!"

His whole body was shaking – "The
thought of you – leaving me – it makes me
shudder with fear!"

Barrington Stoke would like to thank all its readers for commenting on the manuscript before publication and in particular:

Oliver Aarnikoivu
Rachel Almuli
Leo Bichler
Isabel Billig
Madeleine Browne
Hannah Charlton
Caroline Child
Abigail Clemons
William Cope
Lara Cristiano
Sophia Dulenbrook
Julie DeThomas
Ian Dobbins
Charles Ernest
Sarah Gallimore
Jenny Ganer
Alexander Goldberg
Hannah Gronhaug
John Heinrich
Pierre Hientgen
Riley Hoff
Jonathan Holmberg
Shreyam Jalan
Steven Jeffers
Keana Kasinathan
Garrett Kipe

Mateusz Klimkiewicz
Nicholaus Konga
Amelie Kouba
Roman Krawczykowski
Nicholas Lhoest
Steven Nikelski
Rowan MacDonald
Jocelyn McMinimy
Juni Linnea Oldensand
Connor O'Sullivan
Frederik Petersen
Felix Poos
Katherine Reis
Jack Ridgway
Julia Rios
Olle Romlin
Amalie Rosenkvist
Nicholas Ruud
Sara Sacco
Julius Schroeter
Khumayun Shadiev
Saskia Stomph
Kaoru Takayama
Brianna Thomas
Rena Timsit
Molly Vickers
Callum Underwood

Become a Consultant!

Would you like to give us feedback on our titles before they are published? Contact us at the email address below – we'd love to hear from you!

info@barringtonstoke.co.uk
www.barringtonstoke.co.uk

BATTLE CARDS

Daniel Morden

Author

Favourite hero:
Ben Grimm.

Favourite monster:
Grendel's mum.

Your weapon of choice:
The Dental Floss of Doom.

Special secret power:
It's a secret!

Favourite fight scene:
Achilles verses Hector in the Trojan War.

Goodie or baddie:
Every day I try to be a goodie – but sometimes I'm the baddie.

RELOADED

Peter Clover

Illustrator

Favourite hero:
Wolverine from the X-Men!

Favourite monster:
Predator!

Your weapon of choice:
A magical sword.

Special secret power:
Speed!

Favourite fight scene:
Always the one where I win!

Goodie or baddie:
Maybe an inbetweenie! But probably
a goodie!

RELOADED

THE EVIL EYE
BY
OISIN McGANN

Every Halloween, the goblin creeps in from
the Otherworld.

Every Halloween, flesh burns and bodies fall.

The people of Tara need a hero.

Step up Finn MacCool.

He's the only hope they've got …

You can order *The Evil Eye* directly from
www.barringtonstoke.co.uk

WANTED: JANOSIK

BY
ANDREW MATTHEWS

Killer. Thief. Outlaw.
And he's the good guy …
Hero to the poor. Hated by the rich.
Wanted: Janosik.
Dead Or Alive.

THE DRAGON AND THE WARLORD

BY
THOMAS BLOOR

Sheng saw Lord Zuko kill his father.

Now the Warlord is destroying everything.

But there's nothing Sheng can do – until he finds
the dragon's pearl.

Revenge is coming. *Watch the skies ...*

JACK AND THE DRAGON'S TOOTH

BY
LILY HYDE

Welcome to Jack's world.

Where anything can happen and probably will ...

Starring: a wizard, a dragon and a mouse army!

With bonus FUN and added magic.

You can order *Jack and the Dragon's Tooth* directly from
www.barringtonstoke.co.uk

THE GREAT GREEN MONSTER

BY
MAGGIE PEARSON

No one knows where it came from.
And there's no one left to ask – the monster
ate them all.
Akim and his mother are the only people left.
Could anything be worse than the great green
monster?